HENRY'S NIGHT

"Not till we are lost,

in other words not till we have lost the world,

do we begin to find ourselves."

—Henry David Thoreau, "The Village" in *Walden*

FOR ANYA AND CRAIG

Text copyright © 2009 by D. B. Johnson and Linda Michelin
Illustrations copyright © 2009 by D. B. Johnson

Houghton Mifflin Books for Children is an imprint of
Houghton Mifflin Harcourt Publishing Company.

www.hmhbooks.com

The text of this book is set in Bernhard Modern Std.
The illustrations are mixed media.

Library of Congress Cataloging-in-Publication Control Number 2008036113
ISBN-13: 978-0-547-05663-0

Manufactured in China

C&C 10 9 8 7 6 5 4 3 2 1

HENRY'S NIGHT

WRITTEN BY D. B. JOHNSON AND LINDA MICHELIN

ILLUSTRATED BY D. B. JOHNSON

HOUGHTON MIFFLIN BOOKS FOR CHILDREN
HOUGHTON MIFFLIN HARCOURT
BOSTON 2009

July 12

I cannot sleep.

The sounds of the village
keep me awake. The
evening train whistles.
Dogs bark.
And from the room below,
voices drift up to me.

If only I could hear the song
the night bird sings. I take
my collecting jar
and go down the stairs.

Nawshawtuct
Hill

The branches of my beech tree
bend and pull me in.
I sit up to my chin in night
and listen for the bird.

All I hear are berry-pickers
coming home from the hills
and the village bell
tolling—*BONG!*
Nine o'clock.

The night bird
does not sing here.
I slide down from the
tree and leave the village.

Treat treat treat

*Field
Cricket*

Now I walk on the dirt road—

crunch,

crunch,

crunch.

The scuffing of my boots is loud. So I step into a field to listen for the night song.

I hear nothing.

The meadow twinkles with fireflies. They float around me, blinking on and off like shooting stars.

Barn Swallows

½"

I capture fireflies.
They fill my jar
with light.

Nighthawk

A bird swoops
low to my lantern,
and I ask—
Are you the one who sings
the song of night?

Peeent!

Not I, the nighthawk says
as it wings
to the woods.

Campion Flower

I run after,
spilling fireflies as I go.

The village clock strikes ten.

Ten o'clock already.

I stride off into
the woods toward
the rising moon.
I walk on and on as
the moon grows brighter.
There is no path.

Porcupine

3" Quill

Far off I hear
a bird sing,

*Whip-poor-will,
whip-poor-will,
whip-poor-will!*

5 needles

White Pine

There—there is
the song of night.
The bird calls me to follow.

Uphill and down, I follow the
night bird's song. Each time
I get close,
it stops singing.

Now I hear
a pumper bird
gulping water
in the brook.
Which way did the
whippoorwill go? I ask.

American
Bittern

Woonk-ka-chunk, woonk-ka-chunk!
It flew far from the village,
the pumper bird tells me.

So I fill my jar with water
and hike deeper into the woods.
The village clock strikes twelve.

When I hear
the night bird again,
it calls from ahead,
then from behind.
It leads me in circles.

Now it sings from
beyond the hill.
I hurry on to see the bird.
Wait for me, whippoorwill!

A tree root trips me.
My jar rolls away
into a swamp.

Red
Fox

Meadow
Mushroom

I scoop up my jar from the
muddy bottom to see
tadpoles wiggling
in the moonlight.
All around me
frogs croak.
Have you seen

the whippoorwill? I ask.

Trroonk, trroonk!

No one ever sees that bird,
a frog tells me.

Very far away, the village
clock strikes two.

Frog
Eggs

Clouds erase the moon.
Is that thunder I hear?
Raindrops bounce
from my hat.
Lightning
flashes
in my jar.
I leap from
grassy mound to grassy mound
across the swamp.

Rain falls hard now,
but it will not stop me.
Let it pour down—
I will see the bird no one sees.

Raccoon

Hemlock

*3/4"
cones*

Blackberry

Wind blows
me uphill.
Brambles grab my hat
and rain soaks me.
I cannot hear
the bell
in the village anymore.

From a hemlock
tree an owl calls,

Hoo, hoo, hoo-oo.
Who cooks for you?

Owl, I ask, am I lost?
The owl does not say—
so I walk on.

Barred Owl

Dark Eyes

Bracken
Fern

The rain stops.

Here where the woods end,
all is quiet.
I stand on the shore
of a mysterious lake.
White fog spreads wide—
it rolls from edge to edge
of all I see.

How will I get home?

I make a raft of branches
and push off into the mist.

I bend down and scoop
a feather into my jar.

At my back
something flutters,
something sits
on my head.

Whip-poor-will,
whip-poor-will,
whip-poor-will!

it sings into my ear.
The night bird has found me!

I feel the beat of its bird heart.

North Star

Past two islands
I paddle.

The raft, the fog,
the bird's song,
and *I*—
all are as light
as morning air.

The bird leaves me.

A bush poking above
the fog snags my raft.
Down through leaves
I tumble.

Is this the beech tree
in my yard?

I slide down its branches
to the ground.

No one hears me go
up the stairs. I lie in bed
and wait for the noise
of the morning train.
Instead comes a call—

Whip-poor-will,
whip-poor-will,
whip-poor-will! —

the song of night.
The notes flow from my jar
and fill the day with
the night bird's song.

I sleep.

★